The Galactic Saga:

Galactic

Riders

Written and illustrated by
A.C. Winfield

Galactic Riders

ISBN-13: 978-1508733652
ISBN-10: 1508733651

Acknowledgements

Once again, I must say a big thank you to my Mum who is the best!

Also a huge thank you goes to Dominique Goodall for your fantastic editing skills and patience.

A massive thank you to all those of you who have supported me during this process. Be it through facebook, at fairs, events, at work or stopping me in the street. Thank YOU for taking time in your busy day asking me how my books are coming along. It really does mean a lot to me.

Also I would like to say a special thank you to Dolton, Merton and Shebbear pupils for inviting me to their school and for telling me your stories.

And, once again, thanks to you for reading.

THANK YOU!

Ax

I n the deepest, darkest depths of space live
humongous creatures. Some even bigger than
your house, even taller than a skyscraper, dragons!
Yes, dragons. Or as they like to be called, Galactic
Dragons.

These dragons were not your average dragons that
you may find hidden away in dank, dark, icy-cold

caves. No, these dragon are magnificent! Their wings billow in the galactic winds. They soared high above distant planets, their shadows creating eclipses against the burning, bright, brilliant suns.

The Galactic Dragons were also majestic. Zipping through the clouds of galactic dust, leaving a star lit cloud trail behind them.

Their scales were glorious. Though they glittered and glowed in suns, illuminating nebulas and reflecting planets' hue don't let them fool you. Their scales are as hard as iron!

In amongst the vast expanse of space is a tiny blue and green orb, a planet known by its habitants as Earth.

On planet Earth, on a land by the immense blue ocean called the Atlantic Ocean. A little boy called Andrew lived with his mother, father and his older sister, Lou.

Andrew enjoyed the dark. Not only was it fun to play in, enabling him to sneak up on his sister, jumping out shouting "Boo!" and making her jump very high. It also meant the stars and even sometimes the moon were about to come out.

Andrew spent many hours dreaming of what he would be when he was older. Maybe an astrologist? Studying the night sky from way down below while the Milky Way, a glowing band of stars reaching far into outer space. A halo of super novas, red dwarf stars and even supermassive black holes lived up above in the vast, never-ending reaches of space. Or maybe an astronaut! Walking above the Earth's atmosphere. The planet's white, rolling, cotton wool-like clouds churning underneath his dangling, gravity-free feet. Andrew dreamt mostly of being a captain of his own spaceship. Studying distant planets or giant nebulas, giant balls of colourful gas, particles of star dust drifting in the silent depths of space.

Andrew dreamt of many things but never in his wildest dreams did he dream of being a Galactic Rider! This is the story of how this came to be...

Chapter One

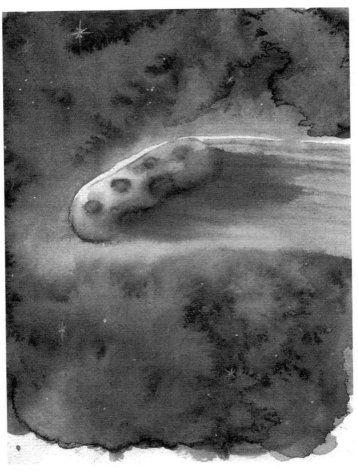

It all began one ordinary evening as Andrew's family sat around the TV. Andrew wasn't really watching, he was too busy playing space monsters and astronauts on the floor until he heard something that caught his attention. "Tonight, an asteroid will narrowly miss the Earth." The news reporter told his captive audience in a very overly dramatic tone.

"Cool!" Andrew whooped and dropped most of his toys onto the floor, before he shuffled closer to the TV. On there was a computer graphic showing an asteroid zooming through space. A big lump of rock with a wispy tail streaming out far behind. "Though we have been reassured the asteroid won't hit Earth, It will only be 3 times the distance from the Earth to the moon."

"But that's so far away!" Andrew told the presenter. Annoyed that he won't have a close encounter with the space rock.

"Andrew. Pipe down!" His sister told him in a very bossy tone.

"Lou, don't be so rude to your brother." Their father told her. Andrew made sure his parents were looking at the TV screen before sticking his tongue out at his sister. She did the same back but he was far more interested in what the reporter had to say next.

"The asteroid has been calculated for reaching

speeds approximately 40,000 miles an hour. You might even be able to see it if you have a telescope or strong pair of binoculars."

Up on the screen now was an actual fuzzy black and white image of the asteroid. "It looks like a dragon to me." Andrew told his family, turning his head and squinting his eyes, shuffling even closer to the screen for a closer look.

"Don't be silly!" His sister told him, nudging her little brother with her foot to get him out the way of the screen.

"Lou!" Both their parents said together, turning to the girl sat between them both.

"But he is being stupid though."

"Lou, if your brother thinks it's a dragon, let him think it's a dragon. It won't harm anyone..." Their father began to say.

Andrew stood up. He was shaking. He felt tears brimming to the surface but he refused to cry. He was angry not upset. "I am not stupid. I was just saying the rock looks like a dragon."

"An asteroid is a lump of rock. So no way can it be a dragon. Besides dragons don't exist." Lou told him, she eyed the dragon Andrew still held in his hand who he was using for a space monster. A sudden roar came from Andrew and before he knew it, he was out the room, slamming the door and running up the stairs to his bedroom.

"Lou, why do you have to be so nasty to your brother? You are the oldest and you are meant to look after him. Not pick on him." Andrew heard his father's voice drift up the stairs. His running feet slowed down slightly at the top of the stairs waiting to hear Lou's response.

"Because he always believes in the impossible. Dragons in space? Really?" With that, there was an almighty bang of a door from upstairs. Andrew had heard enough.

Chapter Two

Andrew's mother came in not long after with a hot cup of hot chocolate and a slice of homemade cake to make her son feel better. She tucked him into bed and kissed him goodnight. As the night grew darker however, Andrew still wouldn't believe the asteroid was just a rock. It was Lou who was the silly one. He would prove it to her. Somehow...

*

Andrew sneaked into his parents' room while they were still downstairs, opened their wardrobe door and took down a big, heavy set of binoculars from the shelving inside. He tiptoed back. The floorboards creaking alarmingly, making him wince for if anyone found out what he was about to do Andrew would be in big trouble.

Andrew waited. Waited and waited for what felt like forever in his bedroom until he heard everyone slink off to bed. He could hear the drum-beat of his sister's music echoing through the darkened landing as she liked to listen to it until she fell to sleep.

With the coast clear and his sister now unable to hear him Andrew got out of bed, put on his astronaut boot slippers, his thick, woolly dressing gown with rockets and galaxies printed on its felted surface and to keep his head warm the boy put on his favourite knitted, bobbled hat, which looked like a green alien.

All set, Andrew picked up the set of binoculars he borrowed earlier and snuck out of his bedroom door. Stepping carefully along the corridor, passing each of his parents' and sister's doors then tiptoed down the stairs as quietly as he could. With a click of a key and a creak of its hinges, Andrew slipped out of the back door. He counted slowly. One, two, three all the way up to ten, nothing. His mum, dad and annoying older sister had not noticed. He breathed a sigh of relief and whipped his head.

Andrew jumped as there was a click and then a light burst to life behind him. Thinking he'd been caught, Andrew whirled around only to find it was only the automatic light sensing his movement. Once again he counted. One, two, three, all the way up to ten. Nothing, the coast was clear. The cooler air bit at his woolly pyjama cladded body. The boy tied his galaxy printed dressing grown tighter around him before unbuckling the binocular case with a loud click! Andrew squirmed. The sound echoed around him loudly. After a few moments of listening and watching the boy eventually took hold of its straps carefully, pulled the binoculars out from their velvet-lined casing and with a soft pop, the twin lenses were revealed.

They were very heavy in Andrew's hands. It was really hard for the boy to hold them up against his eyes but he managed to do it any way. Usually his father helped hold them steady but of course, tonight the lad's father must never know he ever had them.

Andrew frowned. Looking up through the magnifying lenses he could not see the asteroid. He looked around again. He was facing the right direction...Then he remembered the teacher at his school teaching them about light pollution, her voice ringing in his ears.

"The lights from street lamps in our cities, towns and even in the villages can cause light pollution. The light makes it impossible for astrologers or any star gazers to see the stars above."

Maybe it was too light here to see the asteroid? Maybe he needed to try somewhere else, much darker? Andrew looked around for a better spot. He couldn't go to the front of their home. The lane he and his neighbours lived down were full of street lamps.

Another click and his neighbour's back light came on too. Once more Andrew jumped. He didn't want his neighbours to catch him out of bed either. They would only report him to his parents. There was no footsteps however on the other side of the fence so it was most likely due to a passing neighbourhood cat but now there were even more light pollution. Andrew had to get further away. Andrew shook his head. "This won't do at all." It was something his father would have said. As the boy stood, all was quiet apart from the wading birds on the other side of the garden wall. Maybe if he went to the other end of the garden, by the river it would be dark enough to see? There was no lights there but before Andrew had even taken two steps forwards he heard something strange. A kind of faint whistling, whooshing sound. Andrew looked up to where the sound was coming from.

WWHHHOOOOSH!

A multi-coloured giant ball zoomed over the rooftops. The boy's mouth fell open for it was amazing to watch, until he realised it was heading straight towards him! In the last possible moment something unfurled from the ball's sides and with one flap of the multi-coloured arms, the ball skimmed the top of Andrew's head, lifted into the air before pirouetting over the low stone wall. With an almighty splash it crashed into the water beyond making the shore birds go crazy. The white birds rushed out of the marshes and flew away, squawking loudly in alarm.

At first, Andrew was glued to the spot, his heart beating very fast and then, without any more hesitation he ran towards the strange object that had just fallen out of the night sky.

Chapter Three

Andrew ran and ran till his sides hurt. He looked out for any holes dug by the wild rabbits that came into their garden now and again. He did not want to fall down one of those and twist his ankle now he was on an exciting adventure.

Jumping the wall, the lad made his way down to the shoreline. Andrew's mouth fell open. There in front of him, leaping in the water was a huge dragon! Its scales reflecting in the starlight. Their multitude of colours was breath-taking, a few Andrew had never seen before. The dragon was encircling the little red paddle boat he and his father liked to go out in now and again. The scaly creature dived below the rippling waters. Andrew's heart sank. Did he just meet a dragon only for it to disappear once again?

All of sudden the dragon leapt out of the water. Its wings stretching to an enormous size, helping the rainbow coloured lizard-like creature hover for a few seconds before pulling the large wings back into its body once again. With a tumultuous splash, the multi-coloured dragon dived back into the dark water on the other side of the little red, wooden boat.

"Oooohhh." Said Andrew for he realised now the dragon was playing in the water.

Suddenly the dragon turned its head and Andrew stood very still. It was looking right at him! Andrew had heard lots of stories about dragons. Some were fierce, some were friendly but which one was true? Andrew crossed his fingers. "Please be friendly, please be friendly." He wished over and over again. The dragon was coming towards him. Andrew's arms and legs started to shake under the quake of the dragon's gigantic clawed feet as it walked right up to him. The colourful dragon's body raising high above the muddy shore, its talons stirring up the silt. He saw its brilliant array of scales ripple along its body, causing a sound which made Andrew think of one hundred rattle-snakes shaking their tails. Something flicked back and forth through its closed mouth. Like a snake too, smelling its world around his or her-self, the dragon's tongue flicked in and out, in and out. Was this dragon trying to work out how nice little boys tasted as a night time snack?

Andrew was about to turn and run when he saw the dragon's yellow eyes, burning like a rising sun. The dragon may have been gigantic, towering above him. Its scales maybe as loud as one hundred rattle snakes but its eyes were warm and friendly.

Andrew felt his body stop shaking. As he did, so did the dragon's scales. Was this dragon just as afraid as he was? "Hi." Andrew greeted the rainbow coloured dragon. Waving a little, unsure how to greet a dragon. "I'm, I'm Andrew what's your name?" He asked nervously. The dragon's tongue flicked back and forth, its eyes continued to stare down at him. The dragon didn't say anything. "Do you understand me?" He asked nervously. For a moment they continued to look at one another. The rainbow coloured dragon's tongue continued to flick back and forth and then, to Andrew's amazement, the dragon nodded. "Cool! I mean, great!" The dragon grinned its sharp, white fangs which glowed oddly in the light but Andrew only smiled in return. "So," Andrew had so many questions spinning around in his head but there was only one question that he really wished to know. "Where did you come from?" He crossed his fingers very tightly behind his back.

Before Andrew could finish yelling "Whoooa!" The dragon had picked him up by the scruff of his neck, placed him on its back and leapt high into the air. "Where are you taking me?" Andrew shouted over the roar of the wind. The dragon looked back at him, its warm eyes sparkling as it gave a funny kind of laugher. The scales on the front of its face clicked excitedly. Somehow, Andrew knew the dragon was saying "You'll soon see." Higher and higher they climbed till Andrew could reach out and touch the wispy white clouds glowing in the ever-increasing starlight. They passed the clouds and still climbed higher. The dragon's warm body kept Andrew from going cold and even climbing through the clouds, the boy didn't get wet. Was there something magical about this dragon?

Andrew looked up and high above he could see a funny kind of arch way, a hue of blue against the darkness of the night sky, they were leaving the earth's atmosphere! He had learnt all this from his ever increasing number of space books. This was where space began and the world he knew left far behind. "Wait. Wait!" He yelled, banging on the dragon's armoured back trying to get its attention. "There's no air out there! I need it, wait!" All of a sudden it was like the dragon had hit a flexible wall. The dragon pumped its wings even harder, pushing against the blue hued barrier. "No, wait!" Too late. With a tug and a POP! They charge through the barrier and glided off into space.

"What?" Andrew said, unable to believe he was still breathing, warm and also, amazingly, still alive. "How is this possible?"

The dragon's belly shook underneath him. "Because you are with me." Said the dragon. It, Andrew now realised, was a girl dragon. The dragon looked back at Andrew. "My name is Awa." She said. "And you are in the kingdom of the Galactic Dragons now."

*

They glided on in silence for many minutes. Awa's wings flapping now and again. Andrew never noticed before now but Awa's wing's membrane was black with a sheen like oil, reflecting her scales, creating a rainbow effect. Andrew couldn't get enough. He took his time looking around him. Space wasn't dark like Andrew always thought it was. Magical light, like electricity, zipped around them. The sun's light reflecting from the moon beside them cast a turquoise shimmer to the air around them. "Why couldn't you speak before?" Andrew asked, breaking the silence.

"I like your planet that you call Earth. I like visiting, having a swim in your salty seas and clear rivers but…When I first saw you, I thought you were going to hurt me."

"Hurt you?" Andrew couldn't imagine a boy like himself ever being able to hurt a creature such as Awa. Large and powerful with her scales so tough.

Awa nodded. "I never met a human before. We Galactic Dragons are warned not to interact with other beings unless…when I looked into your eyes I knew you would not hurt me. There was a kind of Galactic Dragon feel about you, which I am intrigued about. Would you like to see our world?" Andrew couldn't speak. His head felt like it would explode with all the questions whirling inside. Awa looked back and seeing his expression, smiled a kind smile.

Her teeth glowing in the strange light.

"What's the matter? I do not know much about humans but you seem sad for one riding a Galactic Dragon."

"It's just…" Andrew looked back at the blue and green planet now beneath them. "I knew the asteroid wasn't a lump of rock like everyone was saying. I knew it was a dragon, was it you?" The Galactic Dragon's smile grew wider. Her fangs glittering in the stars' bright light. "When I get back, no one will believe me. My sister will call me silly and think I was lying."

"Well then. We can't have that now, can we?" The multi-coloured dragon asked, as Awa continued to flap her wings, hovering in the star lit space, the flow of electricity softy tickling their skin. "Shall we bring your sister along too?"

"Can we?" Andrew asked excitedly.

"Of course! The more, the merrier. Hold on tight." And he did, wrapping his arms around the giant colourful spike in front of him. Andrew's stomach felt heavy as the Galactic Dragon dived back down to earth. Faster and faster till all around them was fire, its burning heat far away from Andrew in Awa's magical shield. "Ever wondered where comets came from?" Awa looked back at the boy, winking her scaly lidded eye.

"Galactic Dragons?" He asked over the roar of the fire. As he looked back he could no longer see Awa's tail, only fire streaking out far behind.

The Galactic Dragon laughed happily. "Sometimes, and sometimes they are just lumps of rock and ice. Now listen carefully, my young rider. Your sister maybe scared of me when she first sees me so it will be down to you to convince her to come fly with us."

"Ok." Replied Andrew, holding on very tightly to Awa's spike in front of him as Earth's wind buffeted him. "But she is not going to believe me until she has seen you with her own eyes."

Chapter Four

Tap, tap, tap.

Lou sat bolt upright in bed, her music still playing in the background. She was used to the constant drum-beat so what had just woke her up?

Tap, tap, tap.

Was that tapping at the window? She swung her legs around till they dangled over the bed's edge. She slipped her feet into her pink pig slippers. Grabbing her matching dressing gown to keep warm, Lou made her way over to the window. Nervously she took hold of each curtain in each hand.

"Lou?" Did she just hear her name being calling on the other side? "Lou?" Was that her brother's voice? Was this some sort of pay back for earlier? She threw open her curtains ready to tell her brother to stop playing games and go back to sleep but what she saw in front of her made her stop mid-sentence. She couldn't move. Lou stood there, hands shaking while gripping onto the now parted curtains, her mouth gaping.

"Hey Lou." Her brother greeted her, rubbing the

back of his head as he bobbed up and down on the back a multi-coloured, humongous dragon. "Fancy coming for a ride?"

*

It took a lot of persuasion. In the end however Lou convinced herself it was only a dream and that there was no real danger of flying on the back of a giant dragon as it soared off into the sky. That did not stop Lou from wrapping her arms tightly around Andrew's middle, closing her eyes and wishing she was back on earth. As Awa levelled out, she opened her eyes a little bit at a time and what she saw around her made her gasp out loud.

"What? Where are we?" She asked, though she already knew the answer. Below her their home planet, Earth turned on its axis, clouds twirled and spiralled around themselves while above satellites zoomed on by in the star speckled sky as she, Andrew and the rainbow coloured dragon hovered on the spot.

Lou felt and heard both Andrew and the dragon laughing at her. "It's not funny!" She shouted, breathing heavily. Both Awa's bright yellow and Andrew's deep green eyes blinked at her. "Why did I ever agree to this?" She wiped her cheeks, her shaking voice giving away her feelings. "And how are we even breathing?" Lou felt her brother squeezing one of her hands.

She looked at him, expecting her young brother to make fun of her but he was smiling at her kindly. "It's the magic of the Galactic Dragons." He explained.

"Galactic Dragons? Magic?" She asked and he nodded. Lou heard a clattering and as she watched, the scales on the dragon's head moved independently. Awa's tongue flickered in and out. Lou pulled a face. She didn't like snakes much and that's what the flickering reminded her of.

"This is Awa. She's a Galactic Dragon and she's invited us to see her world. Space, Lou!" Her brother smiled broadly, waving his arms around. "Traveling through space on a back of a dragon with magical powers. Come on Lou, please come with me. I have always wanted to see the other planets, the red dwarfs, the ice moon of Jupiter and even black holes! Black holes Lou!" Andrew gave his sister his puppy eyes. She sighed.

"Fine! But I am only agreeing to this because I

know it's all a dream." Lou felt a painful pinch on her arm. "Ow!" She said, rubbing her arm. "What was that for?"

"To prove you aren't dreaming. Do you believe now?" Lou shook her head, her blonde bed head of hair flying out around her. Andrew pulled a face but then he smiled. "Awa, it's all up to you now." Awa gave a gentle laugh.

"Hold on tight young Galactic Riders." Lou's mouth popped open at hearing the dragon speak. Her arms slackened at her sides but she soon snapped out of her stunned silence as Awa pumped her wings and sped forwards, heading into outer space!

Chapter Five

The brother and sister held on very tightly, as Awa pumped her huge leathery wings, zooming along the electric filled sky. Their home planet, now just a turquoise speck in amongst the cluster of stars.

The brother and sister looked at one another. Their thoughts were with their mum and dad they had left far behind but then they grinned. Andrew, had always wanting to go on an adventure, exploring the depths of space and here he was, doing just that and on the back of an enormous, rainbow-coloured dragon. Lou however, still thinking this was a dream knew if she simply woke up she would be safe and sound in her bed. She was kind of enjoying herself so she thought she might as well just sit back and enjoy the view. And what a view it was!

Distant planets, nothing but a pinprick in the night sky now seen with such detail Lou wondered how on earth she was imagining all of this. She was the logical one while her younger brother was the sibling with the heightened imagination. Was it rubbing off? She shook herself. She really hoped not.

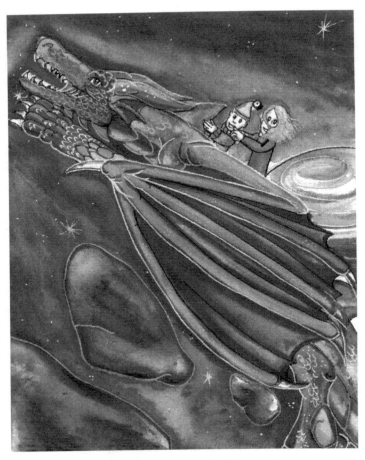

At first the ducking and diving between the asteroids in the asteroid belt was scary. They both screamed as they found themselves spinning, Ava's wings enveloping them, shielding them as she spun through the narrow gaps. Sometimes a rock would ricochet off but her wings were just as hard as the rock and when the wings lifted off them once again, no one was hurt. The two siblings whooped and Awa clicked her scales happily.

"Let's do that again!" Andrew cheered. Lou folded her arms, looking directly at Awa's horned Head.

"Ah, let's not." Awa looked at the two. She was smiling, her strange teeth glowing. Lou noticed Awa did that a lot in the short amount of time that they had travelled together. Looking at the two of them like she was pleased with herself. Lou felt chills go up her arm. "It's just a dream Lou." She muttered to herself as she rubbed her arms.

Just then Awa's wings became taut, like a sail catching a strong breeze. "Hold on tight." Awa cried back. "This might get a little bumpy." She tilted her reflective wings, a sheen shone across them similar to oil on water and just like that, they sped forwards.

Lou screamed till her lungs hurt, gripping onto her brother very tightly but Andrew being Andrew, held on with just one hand while punching the air with the other. "YEAH!" He yelled. Lou closed her eyes very tightly. "Andrew!" She yelled at him. "Stop showing off and just hold on, will ya?"

"Fine." He sighed, his voice barely audible over

the howling noise as they sped along the strange current. If she had her eyes open, Lou would have rolled them at her younger brother. He was even annoying in her own dreams.

"Awa, what is this place?" She heard her brother asking. His voice sounded strange, far away. Little by little Lou opened her eyes again and gasped. If this was a dream, then her imagination was definitely getting out of control!

Around them, particles of some kind flew past at incredible speed till they were streams of multiple colours. It was the fact that they were not rushing past them from the front to back but the other way round that shocked her. The coloured lines changing now and again, some even danced with one another as they filled the dragon's wings, pushing the three of them forwards at an incredible speed. The lines surrounding them waved up and down, allowing Lou to see between them but she couldn't make anything out. They were going way too fast and watching the bands made her feel ill, like car sickness when you've kept your eyes on the lines. She turned back around, looking ahead. Her breath caught again. In front was a stunning sight. A bright star surrounded by other streams, connecting, flowing to this one central point like tributaries adjoining a river.

"This is Eridanus, the river of the solar winds. We Galactic Dragons use it to sail our way across the solar system. The star in front is home to many of our kind. Welcome to Eridani."

Chapter Six

Eridani was nothing like either the brother or sister had seen before. Lou had to keep hold of Andrew so he wouldn't jump off Awa's back, running off to explore their surroundings. The ground was like frosty coloured crystal but with a lattice of electricity running through it. They landed on what seemed to be pasture where strange cow-like creatures with six legs and horns roamed freely. Lou figured they must be used to dragons landing here, for they didn't become startled by their sudden presence. In the distance a great city rose up. Many skyscrapers of diamond like crystals glittered in the Rainbow Rivers' light. There was no sun here but the dragon's multi-coloured streams and planet's energy running through the ground beneath their feet seemed to be enough to light the world around them.

As the three entered the city, they were joined by other travellers. Other dragons. Andrew thought Awa was big but compared to the many of those around them, she was tiny and he and Lou were like ants! "It is safer if you stay on my back." Awa told them. Lou's grip slackened around her brother's waist as she took the city in. The skyscrapers were like none on Earth but were more like honeycombs, full of hexagon openings. Some big enough for the likes of Awa while others were big enough to hold a whale and more. "It's like a hive!" Andrew said out loud and as if hearing him a black and yellow dragon, with bee-like wings flew past and crawled inside its hollowed den.

Now and again a humanoid figure would walk past, bowing his or her head or even heads at the two children. "It's rude to stare." Lou reminded her brother as he gawped but for once she didn't blame him. If she was standing from afar, she was sure she was being just as rude.

Each of the figures were clad from head to toe in blue and silver uniforms. Some of these people were nearly as tall as the dragon the brother and sister rode, the rider's hand on their companion's shoulder. Each one had their hoods up, casting dark shadows over their faces. Without seeing their faces, it was impossible for Andrew or Lou to know if there were any other humans on this planet. Lou's hairs once again stood up on end. Was this dream now turning into a nightmare?

Now and again a figure would stand out from the crowd. Clad all in red and gold. Everyone seemed to be hurrying in the same direction. "Awa, where you taking us?" Awa looked back at Lou intently, for once the Galactic Dragon's eyes looked sad. She looked at the girl, then at Andrew and back again.

"Up there." She sighed, her gaze now on the tallest of all the hive-like skyscrapers standing in what seemed to be the city's centre. Both Lou and Andrew stared. Wrapping themselves around the corners of the huge, crystal building, two multi-coloured lines spiralled their way to the top. "The Galactic Dragons and their riders are waiting for us." Only now did the brother and sister see the different colours were moving, two separate lines of dragons and their riders, clad top to toe in their strange outfits. One line had red and gold while the other had blue and silver uniforms. None of the dragons or their riders were flying to the top but instead climbing the spiral, open aired staircases.

"Why?" Lou asked. Awa sighed, wisps of fire licking the edges of her mouth.

"Because we have been summoned."

*

The silence in the arena was deafening. Andrew twitched where he stood and Lou, standing beside him, her ears were ringing and the hairs on the back

41

of her neck could not had stood any more up right. She pinched herself, over and over again. "Wake up Lou." She begged herself, but she was beginning to come to the conclusion that maybe this was not a dream after all, and that she could no longer escape what was turning from a dream into a nightmare. Andrew started jumping on the balls of his feet. She knew he was just as nervous as she was. Lou took her brother's hand and squeezed, trying to calm him.

In front of them rows and rows of Galactic Dragons and their riders sat, watching the three closely. One side was riders dressed in red and gold while the other, riders dressed in blue and silver. In front of the children sat two dragons beside them, their riders sat in cut crystal chairs made from the same entity as the city. Crystal with lines of electricity running through them, like veins in a dragon's wing.

"Awa, what's going on?" Andrew whispered to the rainbow coloured dragon for what felt like the hundredth time to Lou, the dragon however wasn't looking at them now but at the floor. Was it just Lou or did she look frightened as well? Not good.

"Welcome." The dragon with the blue and silver rider greeted them at last. Their riders were the only ones without hoods shadowing their faces. The blue and silver rider was female, like her dragon and had bright blue skin and light silvery blond hair, her dragon, who had spoken, had purple fur which grew longer down around her neck till they tipped with white, fanning out into a mane. Lou thought she looked pretty, while the other dragon looked foreboding. The dragon on the left, on the side with red and gold riders was dark silver in colour. Horns protruded all along his jaw line and neck where his hard skin overlapped one another. This dragon's skin reminded her of the armoured plating she had seen in dinosaur books. The horns continued down his spine till it ended in a deadly shard at the tip of his tail He had red patterns painted on his cheeks and flank. Along his back was an impressive saddle. There were all kinds of hooks and loops ready to hold something but whatever they were, they were all gone. Lou shivered, she had a feeling she did not want to know. Beside the powerful, dark silvered dragon was his or her rider. This time a male, red skin and bald head.

He had powerful a jaw and just like his dragon's, had piercings up along the bridge of his nose and along the line of his jaw. Metal spikes.

"Welcome." The dark dragon leered, his eyes making the children's hearts stop for just a moment. This dragon was male and he looked and sounded like he was ready to eat them alive.

"Ahren, be gentle on our new riders. They will be judged fairly and a solution will be found."

Lou's and Andrew's mouth fell. Judged! Lou turned to Awa, who squirmed on the spot, Lou didn't know what Awa was doing but it looked like she was trying to make herself as small as possible. The sound coming from her made Lou feel sick.

There was a murmur of words rising from the stands. Lou didn't look, she could feel Andrew's hand shaking in her own. She continued to watch Awa, who now lay on the floor, her bright yellow eyes only for her own green. *Forgive me.* Lou gasped. Awa's voice was in her own head.

"Silence!" Ahren cased his burning red eyes around the stands and then at Awa.

"Awa," It was the purple dragon who now spoke. "You will refrain from using your telekinesis in this court. Unlike your riders, you know the rules." A low submissive rumble came from the rainbow dragon, her scales rattling like barley in a strong breeze.

"Let's start again." Ahren puffed a plume of smoke as dark as his armour from his snout. Both he and the purple-furred dragon looked at one another, their riders in their uniforms not moving but continued to watch on. One smiling kindly at the two

45

children while the other sneered as deadly as his dragon. "Aura?" The dark silver dragon addressed the other Galactic Dragon sat beside him and spread out his clawed paw gesturing for her to speak. Aura bowed her furry head gracefully and turned to the children before her.

"Greetings, Galactic Riders." It took a while for the brother and sister to realise it was them who were being addressed. "Welcome to the halls of Eridani, home of the Eridan's Galactic Dragons and their riders. As you can see, your presence has created a stir amongst our two clans." The children frowned.

"Of course," Aura continued, as though understanding the many questions running through their minds. "I should start from the beginning. As you can see, we Galactic Dragons are not alone. Each one is destined to have a Galactic Rider. A dragon cannot reach full maturity, their powers cannot grow without their...what would you humans call such a partnership? Soulmate?" The children continued to frown. Though Lou, the eldest of the two understood, it did not mean she liked where this was going. "However saying all this, a human rider has not been claimed before, let alone two riders for one dragon. Awa, speak, tell us how you had chosen your riders." There was an almighty sound, a rumble like thunder as hundreds of shifting bodies clad in leather, scales, feathers and fur turned, all eyes focusing now on the rainbow coloured dragon. Her back arched, reminding Lou of a frightened cat backed into a corner.

"I," Lou watched on as her tongue flicked in and out nervously. "I," She tried again.

"Speak up!" Ahren's rider bellowed across the immense arena.

"I was traveling through the far reaches of space known as the Milky Way." Her eyes flicked back and forth between the children. Lou's eyebrows came down even further. Distrust stirred within her. "As I was told since I was just a hatchling, I felt the pulling to a planet called by its habitants, Earth." Andrew let go of Lou's clammy hand now and made his way over to the terrified dragon. He lay his hand attentively on Awa's shoulder and as they looked at one another, Lou watched Awa's hunched back lower slightly. "I am so sorry." The dragon's words reflecting her tone of voice.

"For what?" Andrew asked but she merely shook her head before continuing. "I felt the pull of my rider." She continued. Her eyes now only for the humans stood beside her but loud enough so the whole crowd could hear. "I saw Andrew and knew he was the one. My Galactic Rider I was destined to fly with for the rest of my life. When we flew the connection was complete, I could feel the power coursing its way through my veins but I still felt a pull. When he told me about his sister," The dragon's yellow eyes flew over to Lou's now, transfixing her to the spot. "I thought maybe she had the answer. With the two of them, I felt complete. My body surging with new powers. Even though I was taught about the change, I could not have imagined how complete I felt but..." She stopped, smoke starting to billow from her scaly nose.

"But what?" Lou asked, her voice sounding not so friendly now. She was shaking again but not through nervousness but because she was angry. Had she and her brother been lied to all this time? "But what?" She asked again through clenched teeth. There was laughter. A menacing kind of laughter that pierced your heart till it stopped beating. It wasn't just one person who was laughing, but two. Ahren and his rider was laughing harmoniously.

"Why don't you tell her Awa? I am sure this little human you chose is dying to know." Ahren licked his lips. Lou shivered. She marched over to Andrew and taking his arm, dragged him out of reach of the rainbow coloured dragon. Andrew protested but she didn't let go. Whatever was going on she did not like it.

"Andrew, please stop." Lou's voice sounded flat and breathless. Not like her usual self at all. Andrew instantly stopped tugging to get away from his sister but looked back and forth between her and his new friend, Awa. He looked bewildered. "Tell me." Lou breathed, her voice so quiet but knew the dragons and their riders could hear with their sharp ears. Awa's glowing, yellow eyes never left the girl's.

"Each dragon and his or her rider is an echo of one another." Awa began. "As you can see in front of us, blue and silver for those who live on Eridani in the Eridanus quadrant. They feed on pure star light while the red and gold, they live on Epsilon, feeding on

49

Dark Matter. Light and dark." The dragon simplified. Watching Lou and her brother closely, making sure they understood the light and dark didn't just mean the dragons' and their riders' source of power. "It has always been this way since the beginning of the universe. A Galactic Dragon was never on one side or the other until their rider is found…" It was Andrew's turn now to take hold of Lou's hand as she shook. Giving her fingers a little squeeze.

"Lou?" He said, his eyes big and shiny. "Lou, what does Awa mean? I don't understand."

Lou shook her head. "No."

"Yessss." The red man hissed. Only now did they see it wasn't only his studs reflecting his dragon's accruements but also his 'v' shaped tongue. "Eridan's breathe life. Epsilons end it. The balance of life in the universe is delicate. One life form could tip the other's existence and it is our task to judge which should live and which will be extinguished. Now tell me little Andrew," The red man stood up from his chair and making his way over to the two children. His Galactic dragon watched on where he sat. "Tell us what colour you see in this world's crystal and throughout the universe?"

Andrew frowned, pressing up against his sister whose body was still shaking. "Why do you want to know that?" He asked the man with the bald head and skin as red as if he had stood in the sun for far too long.

"Don't answer him, Andrew." Lou told her brother, putting herself between Andrew and the red skinned rider.

"It's a simple question, young human. Please answer." It was the lady with the bright blue skin that now spoke. Her dragon watched the child carefully.

"But everyone can see the same colour...can't you?" He looked up at his sister whose eyes were now shedding tears but she looked more annoyed than upset, glaring at the red rider. "It's blue."

The man and Ahren hissed, looking very annoyed. The blue lady and her dragon however looked pleased as though their dreams were coming true but it was Lou Andrew was still looking up at. He knew that look, it was the look she had when he came into her room without permission.

"Young lady, the same question." Aura asked, her

crystal blue eyes glittering but Lou pursed her lips, nibbling them nervously.

Awa? She thought. Hoping this would work. *Awa?*

Yes. Came the dragon's voice inside her head. Lou tried not to wince at the intrusion of another being inside her mind.

Can you escape? With Andrew and me?

Awa didn't reply but her gaze said it all.

"Awa, this is your second warning." Ahren announced in a bored but clear tone so the crowd could hear the announcement. "Now young human. Answer the question." There was a very long pause. Lou's heart drummed in her ears, rattling her ear drum.

NOW! Lou thought as loud as she could, hoping Awa would hear.

Chapter Seven

Andrew yelled as he was grabbed by Awa. Her
talons closing around him securely while Lou
pounded towards the rainbow coloured dragon and
leapt high into the air, landing safely (though not

quite lady-like) on Awa's scaly back. Was that adrenaline kicking in or something else? She had no time to ponder. With both on safely board, the Galactic Dragon bent her armoured knees and spread her wings. With one mighty downward flap, she sailed up into the sky.

Down below the crowd roared. Ahren, Aura and their riders loudest of all. "Awa! You have broken so many laws and now you have broken your clans' trust." Ahren's voice rose up to them. "If you return now, you and your riders will be forgiven."

"No, they won't." Awa called down to the dark silvered, heavily armoured dragon. "You just want them to fight your stupid wars."

"Awa, what are you doing? Flee!" Lou shouted over the voices. The dragons' hot breaths as they gazed up at them made her skin turn as red as Ahren's rider's.

"They won't fly after us while they are still in the auditorium." Awa told her. "If any of them do, it'll break the peace treaty between their clans."

"But haven't you already broken that treaty?" Lou wished she could move the dragon's wings herself.

As she wished, a strange feeling spread over her whole body and for a moment, she could see through Awa's eyes. Everything was in sharper focus, each of the dragons and their riders seemed much closer somehow and round them, a light emitted from their bodies. Some blue and some red. Each Galactic Rider connected to their dragon. The same light that ran through the universe and the crystal planet.

Awa shook her horny head. *Not now Lou.* She told her gently and just as though she flicked an elastic band, the connection snapped, leaving Lou trying to catch her breath. *And not quite. You understand now don't you? Somehow I have connected to two riders. You and your brother. Each of you connected to one side.*

"I am not on anyone's side!" Lou corrected her aloud.

Precisely. Right now you see red energy but what will stop you from seeing blue as well? You are not trained, you are unstable. There has never been a human rider before so who knows the powers we can have together and you two are an anomaly, a new kind of rider that could tip the balance of the clans and the existence of the universe itself.

So you didn't care to tell us?

I am sorry. I didn't mean for it to get so complicated. I was nervous and excited at finally meeting my new riders and discovering our new powers that I let it blind me to see the truth of why the clans were summoning us. I am trained by both sides in what to expect when I receive my new powers, how to train together with my new rider. Our riders choose who we are. There's no questions asked for it is our nature but now...

We have changed that, my brother and I. Tipping the balance?

Not quite, you still haven't picked a side.

"But I don't want to pick a side!" Lou bellowed, annoyed at the repeated statement.

Precisely, and so neither do I. Lou's head was too full of questions to understand.

"Lou, what are we doing up here?" She heard her brother's voice from far below.

"Andrew." She breathed, looking over the side of the dragon. For a few moments she had completely forgot he was still being held by Awa but maybe that was the safest place. Protected by Awa's tough scales rather than being exposed on the back of her, looked on by beings that can launch fire balls and whatever else they can shoot from their mouths. "Just hold on till we work this out, ok?" Andrew nodded but she could see he didn't quite understand what was going on.

"If you three have quite finished." Ahren spoke up to them. "What's it going to be Awa? Are you coming down so that you and your riders can finally choose their rightful clan or do they need help choosing?" Lou felt Awa's heart beat quickened with her own. So is that the Epsilon's plan? If she and her brother didn't choose their side together, Andrew would be taken away so Aura's clan would claim him and Ahren's would claim her? But what about Awa? She couldn't be on both sides, could she? Lou's head started to hurt.

"I will choose!" Awa cried. A deafening roar erupted below but Awa vanished in a blink of an eye. She soared out to the nearest multi-coloured stream, spread her enormous shimmering wings, catching the solar winds.

"Where we going?" Lou breathed, trying to calm herself down so she could think of a plan.

I am taking you back home. The reply rang in the girl's head.

Why? Maybe... Lou thought of a plan of taking Andrew back home, she and Awa then can fly off. The Epsilons and Eridans will follow them instead while Andrew would be hidden at home.

Awa shook her head. *No good. If any of them find Andrew alone, it'll be easy to kill him or claim him. At least together you two can stay hidden.*

How?

Awa sighed with a heavy heart, so much so flames licked her nose and a rattle coursed its way down her scaly body. *You have to forget me.*

"NO!" Lou yelled out loud.

"Lou? Are you ok? Where are we going?" She heard Andrew's small voice from down below but she couldn't look at him. If she looked as terrified as she felt...

Yes, you must. Lou heard Awa's voice once again. As well as her voice, she felt a sort of weight there now, in the back of her mind. As Lou blinked she saw

Awa's multi-coloured face but somehow she didn't find it scary, she found it comforting. *I must take you two back home, to Earth before your powers grow too strong. If we split up, if I fly far enough away it will lessen. The clans will track me instead, thinking we are still together. Riders and their dragons are meant to be one. They wouldn't expect it.*

But what about you? Lou asked, wiping her face.

It will be painful but I can do it, if it means both of you are safe.

*But...*Lou tried thinking up excuses, anything to not to lose Awa. Strange that not that long ago she was terrified of being on the back of a dragon, thinking it was all but a dream and now, now she was terrified of it being so. Even if it meant her life...

Lie.

Sorry? Lou frowned, utterly confused at what Awa was telling her after so many mixed emotions.

Lie to yourself and your brother. Convince yourself meeting me was all but a strange dream and convince your brother too. Without the connection, our powers will lessen and so the clans cannot detect you. Lie to keep yourselves safe. I will not allow either of the clans to claim you. If they do I do not know what will happen... There was complete silence between the two. Physically or through telekinesis. Terrifying images filling their minds that they did not wish to share. Lou knew her friend was right but it would mean losing her, forever. *Please.* Awa pleaded.

More tears tumbled their way down Lou's cheeks now but through all the fog in her brain, she knew Awa was making sense. This was the only way...for now. She took a few steady breaths, wiped her face before leaning over Awa's side so her brother could see her. "It's ok Andrew, we're going home."

"Awa too!" He asked, beaming. She cringed on the inside. Though the presence of Awa had now left her, she still heard her voice. *Lie.*

Chapter Eight

Awa hovered in front of Andrew's bedroom window, the automatic light outside clicking on. Lou found it strange to be back down to earth, quite literally.

"I don't want to say goodnight." Andrew told Awa as he hugged her tightly around her armoured head as she placed the young boy gently on his bed.

"Come on, Andrew." Lou tugged his sleeve, trying to pull him away. She couldn't look the dragon in the eye, afraid that she will crumple. Lou helped her brother out of his sodden slippers, muddy dressing gown and pulled off his alien bobbled hat before tucking him in.

"But I don't want Awa to go."

"We'll see her again in the morning." Lou's lie made her insides squirm. The lad rubbed his eyes, yawning widely.

"Promise?" He asked Lou and Awa. His drooping eyes toing and froing between the two of them.

"Promise." Lou and Awa said at the same time. Their gazes met, eyes wide. Lou felt it in their hearts they both hated lying to her brother but it wasn't the lie that frightened them the most, it was the connection. It was getting stronger.

"I must go." And before Andrew or even Lou could call her back, Awa spread her wings and took off. Lou ran to the window, her tangled hair even more so as the wind from the dragon's wings buffeted her. As she watched, Awa's rainbow form vanished into the electric night. Lou's heart sank. If she could see the electricity, how was their lie ever going to work?

"Lou?" Andrew yawned.

"Yes?" Lou replied, her voice breaking despite her best efforts. She rubbed her chest, it ached. She waited for her brother's next question but it never came. As she turned, Lou found her brother fast asleep. His one arm drooped across his face, while the other stretched out stretched over the edge. His mouth wide open as soft snores escaped it. Despite her aching heart and the painful feeling of loss, Lou smiled down at her sleeping brother. "Dummy." She said shaking her head and left the room, clicking the door softly closed behind her.

Before heading to bed herself Lou headed downstairs. She stuffed her pink pig and Andrew's astronaut boot slippers into the washing machine, along with her pink and Andrew's galaxy printed dressing gown. She also locked the back door and after making sure the timer was still on, so the washing machine came on as their mother had originally planned, she headed upstairs to bed.

Lou closed her eyes and just for a moment allowed her thoughts to drift off into space one last time. In front of her lay maybe the only formation she recognised from her brother's space books, the

Horsehead Nebular. It had always been her favourite. The horses head a dark, cloudy mass in front of a radiating pink abundance of light. Above and below, the stars shone brighter than ever before. The solar winds whispering loudly in her ears.

"Goodnight Awa." She whispered just as sleep was about to embrace her.

Goodnight Lou. I will miss you both.

The End

Ebony's Legacy:

Book 1: The Star Pirate
Book 2: The Comet Cat
Book 3: On its way!

The Galactic Saga:

Book 1: Galactic Riders
Book 2: On its way!

About the Author

A.C. Winfield (Amy) lived in St.Ives (Porthia) on the west coast of Cornwall, England, for the past 21 years. She now, however, lives in north Devon where most of her influences come from.

At secondary school she was diagnosed with slight dyslexia, which made English and exams a struggle, but determined, she managed to get the GCSEs needed for her college course.

After leaving school, Amy studied an NVQ in photography, and continued her passion for this and art by selling her work at local fairs and events, while sharing her enthusiasm for art with children at schools and clubs.

Since 2006, Amy has had the land of Ia (looking a lot like the outline of Cornwall with influences from north Devon's landscape) floating around and forming inside her head. Characters, creatures and places soon followed the story told to her by Stella.

Along with Stella came Ebony and her legacy.

Amy now uses her artistic and photographic skills to create covers and illustrations for other authors, as well as completing her own children's books.

Made in the USA
Lexington, KY
24 May 2018